WELCOME TO
PASSPORT TO READING
A beginning reader's ticket to a brand-new world!

Every book in this program is designed to build read-along and read-alone skills, level by level, through engaging and enriching stories. As the reader turns each page, he or she will become more confident with new vocabulary, sight words, and comprehension.

These PASSPORT TO READING levels will help you choose the perfect book for every reader.

READING TOGETHER
Read short words in simple sentence structures together to begin a reader's journey.

READING OUT LOUD
Encourage developing readers to sound out words in more complex stories with simple vocabulary.

READING INDEPENDENTLY
Newly independent readers gain confidence reading more complex sentences with higher word counts.

READY TO READ MORE
Readers prepare for chapter books with fewer illustrations and longer paragraphs.

This book features sight words from the educator-supported Dolch Sight Words List. This encourages the reader to recognize commonly used vocabulary words, increasing reading speed and fluency.

For more information, please visit passporttoreadingbooks.com.

Enjoy the journey!

Little, Brown and Company

Hachette Book Group
1290 Avenue of the Americas, New York, NY 10104
Visit our website at lb-kids.com

Little, Brown and Company is a division of Hachette Book Group, Inc. The Little, Brown name and logo are trademarks of Hachette Book Group, Inc.

The publisher is not responsible for websites (or their content) that are not owned by the publisher.

First Edition: April 2014

Library of Congress Cataloging-in-Publication Data

Jakobs, D. (Devlan), 1974–
  Meet Blades the copter-bot / adapted by D. Jakobs ; based on the episode "Under Pressure" written by Nicole Dubuc.
    pages cm. — (Passport to reading. Level 1)
  "Transformers Rescue Bots."
  ISBN 978-0-316-18870-8 (pbk)
  I. Dubuc, Nicole, 1978- II. Transformers, Rescue Bots (Television program) III. Title.
  PZ7.J1535545Me 2014
  [E]—dc23

                                          2013029888

10 9 8 7 6 5 4

CW

Printed in the United States of America

Passport to Reading titles are leveled by independent reviewers applying the standards developed by Irene Fountas and Gay Su Pinnell in *Matching Books to Readers: Using Leveled Books in Guided Reading*, Heinemann, 1999.

Licensed By:

TRANSFORMERS® RESCUE BOTS

Meet Blades the Copter-Bot

Adapted by **D. Jakobs**

Based on the episode
"Under Pressure" written by
Nicole Dubuc

LITTLE, BROWN AND COMPANY
New York Boston

Attention, Rescue Bots fans!

Look for these items when you read this book.

Can you spot them all?

HELICOPTER

VOLCANO

LAVA

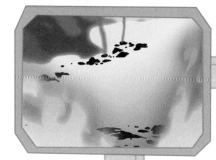

SWITCH

Earth is very strange to the Rescue Bots.

Blades is having a hard time
in his new home.

On Cybertron, Blades was a land vehicle.

He had wheels!

But here on Earth,

he changes into a helicopter.

Helicopters do not ride on the ground.

They fly!

Blades is scared of heights!

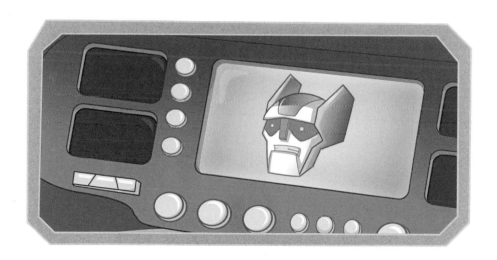

Blades has to be brave and fly
so he can do what
Optimus Prime told him.

Blades's human partner, Dani, loves to fly.

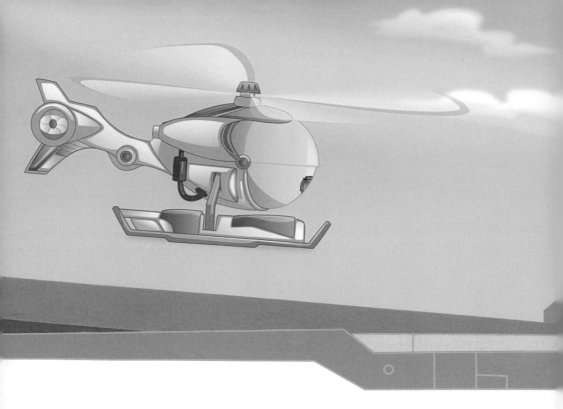

When they are flying together,

she pulls hard at his controls and yells at him.

"Hurry up, Blades!" she says.
"Go higher!"

Cody gets his family and the Rescue Bots together in the bunker.

He wants them to like and respect one another.

Blades and Dani try to be friends.

"Er, do you have any hobbies?" asks Blades.

"Flying," says Dani.

Blades does not like this answer.

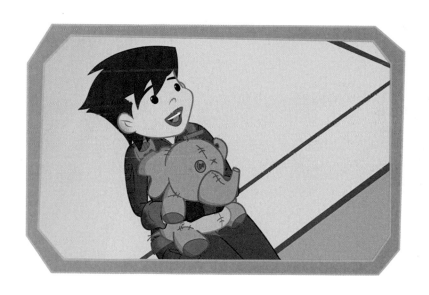

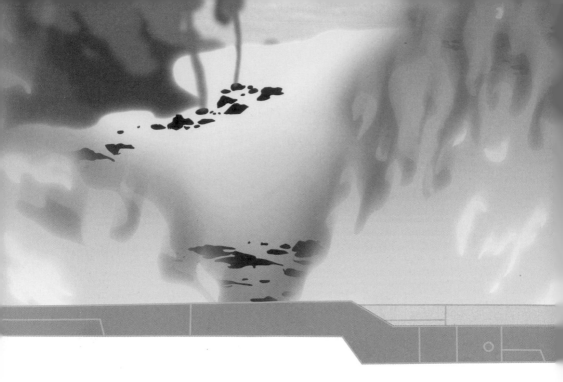

Just then, the town's fake volcano
starts erupting real lava!
Lava is rock that is so hot, it flows.
It can burn anything in its path.

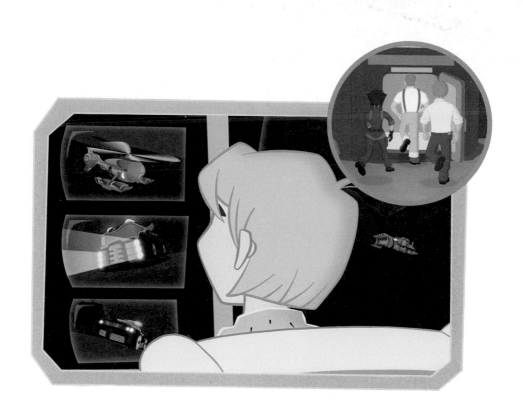

The team leaps into action.

Blades and Dani need to fly into the crater
and flip a switch before the volcano explodes.

"Ow!

Can you be more gentle?" asks Blades.

"As soon as you learn to fly," says Dani.

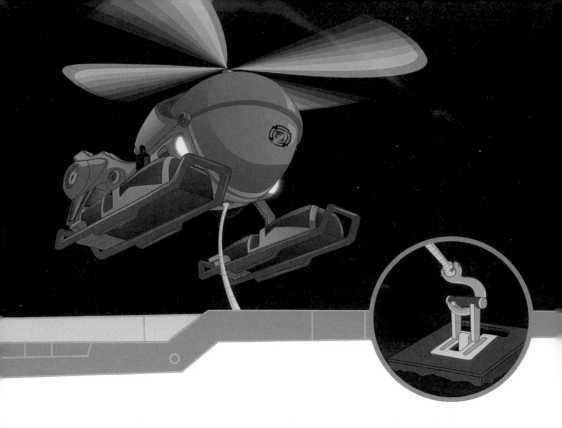

They need to fly fast and high.
The flying is scarier to Blades
than the lava, but he flips the switch!

"We did it!" says Dani.

BOOM!

A cloud of ash bursts from the volcano.

Blades cannot see a thing!

"Fly higher!" yells Dani.

"Which way is higher?" says Blades.

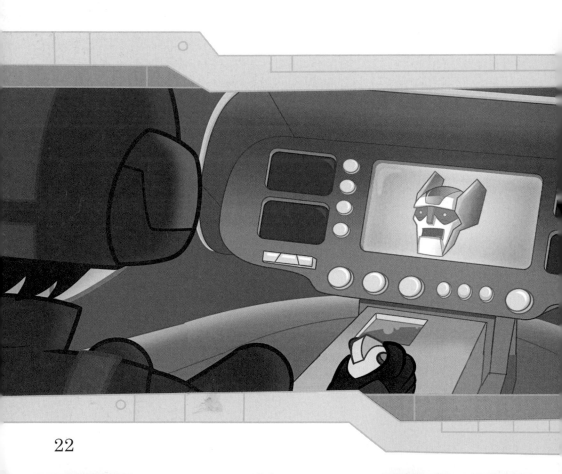

"Talk nicely to Blades, Dani,"
says Cody from the command center.

Dani and Blades work together
to get away from the ash and lava.
They are happy,
but the emergency is not over.

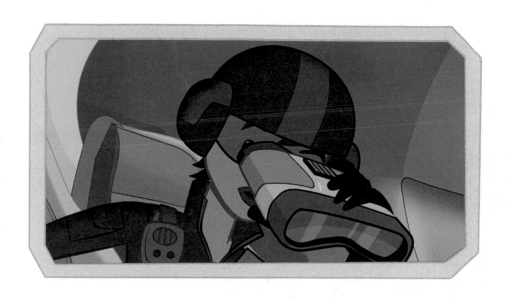

The leftover lava is heading down the tunnels toward Cody!

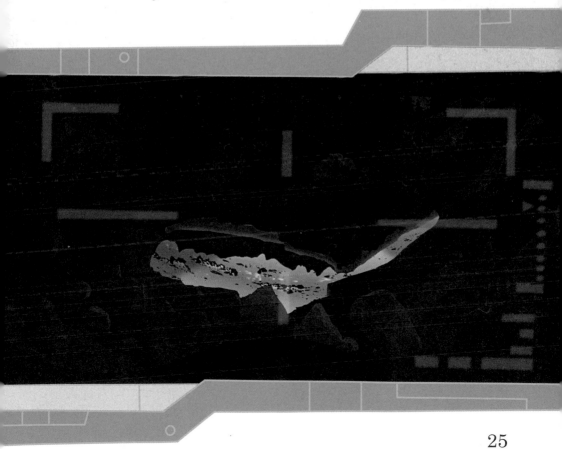

They need to cool the lava
and turn it back into rock quickly!

Heatwave and Kade try to stop the lava,
but the tanks run out of water.

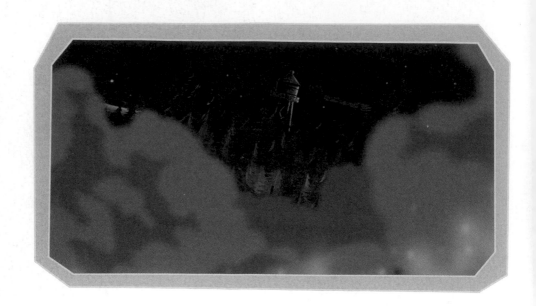

There is a huge water tower nearby,
but the ash cloud is in the way.
Only Blades can get there in time.

"The ash may hurt your rotors," says Dani.

"It is worth it to help Cody!" says Blades.

With Dani's help,
Blades soars through the smoke
and picks up the water tower.
Together, they save the day.

"We did it, partner!" says Dani.

They both feel very proud.

Blades finally feels at home.